Annotations

For My Parents

Annotations

1995

John Keene

A NEW DIRECTIONS BOOK

Copyright © 1995 by John Keene

All rights reserved. Except for brief passages quoted in a newspaper, magazine, radio, or television review, no part of this book may be reproduced in any form or by any means, electronic or mechanical, including photocopying and recording, or by any information storage and retrieval system, without permission in writing from the Publisher.

Acknowledgments: Grateful acknowledgment is made to the editors and publishers of magazines in which sections of *Annotations* first appeared: *Callaloo, Eyeball, Hambone, The Kenyon Review,* and *o.blek*.

Author's Note: Thanks are due to the Artists Foundation of Massachusetts and the Massachusetts Cultural Council, whose Fellowship partially supported the creation of this work.

Manufactured in the United States of America
New Directions Books are printed on acid-free paper
First published as New Directions Paperbook 809 in 1995
Published simultaneously in Canada by Penguin Books Canada Limited

Library of Congress Cataloging-in-Publication Data

Keene, John.
   Annotations / John Keene.
     p. cm. — (New Directions paperbook ; 809)
   ISBN 0-8112-1304-8 (alk. paper)
   1. Afro-American families—Missouri—Saint Louis—Fiction.
2. Afro-American youth—Missouri—Saint Louis—Fiction. I. Title.
PS3561.E3717A82   1995
813'.54—dc20   95-23526
                                                                                                         CIP

New Directions Books are published for James Laughlin
by New Directions Publishing Corporation,
80 Eighth Avenue, New York 10011

SECOND PRINTING

Annotations

I

JUST AS DROWNING IS SAID TO BE DELICIOUS
WHEN ONE STOPS STRUGGLING,
SO I TRIED TO REPRODUCE THAT DELICIOUS SENSATION.
John Ashbery

WHAT MEMORY IS NOT A "GRIPPING" THOUGHT.
Lyn Hejinian

EVERYTHING COMES TOGETHER IN A NOVEL,
LIFE IS ANOTHER MATTER.
Clarence Major

Notes, Inscribed Initially in the Narrow, Running Margin

Such as it began in the Jewish Hospital of St. Louis, on Fathers' Day, you not some babbling prophet but another Negro child, whose parents' random choices of signs would disorient you for years. It was a summer of Malcolms and Seans, as Blacks were transforming the small nation of Watts into a graveyard of smoldering metal. A crueler darkening, as against the assured arrival of dusk. Selma-to-Montgomery. Old folks liked to say he favored the uncle who died young, an artist. In that way, a sense of tradition was upheld, one's place in the reference-chain secured. Digression. Brick houses uniform as Monopoly props lined the lacework of street for miles. Before there was Arlington, there was Palm, indeed a dimmer entity which burns in one's memory like iodine. "Baltimore Law." They eventually settled on a single-family detached, in the Walnut Park section of the city, after months of wrangling with the agent, as it was quite naturally assumed that they, like others who worked for a living, would eventually own their own property. The red cement porch, which Daddy painted at least one time, beneath the gray-greenish, slate-shingled eaves. The draperies had not yet begun to rot, nor had the ottoman relinquished a leg to leaning. Some of them were working at the post office then, though many were unionized auto-plant or factory workers. Cleverness in conformity often goes unnoticed. The block opened out onto the immense Calvary Cemetery that we had heard to be the haunt of vampire mummies, who would lie in wait beneath the headstones for children who failed to say their prayers. In the mirror, an admirer. You dreamed of romping there when older with the tougher boys, smoking cigarettes, copping feels, jumping out from behind trees, playing like an agent from "Dragnet." Crossing the street was considerably more forbidding. Four, in hand. A home in which to watch the seasons pass, to grow old within a chosen "community." Now names of most neighbors have shifted past his consciousness like afternoon shadows across the living room floor. Everyone, except the neighbors, marveled at the size of the basement. Then no one used heroin because they lacked for "family values," even though they spoke so blithely of our "ghetto." Pruitt-Igoe. Words, wildly uttered, acts unmitigated, emergence of their search for validation. Many backyards wore a chain-link garter that stretched out to the alleyway, and so whenever the rudipoots shattered their wine or soda bottles into smithereens of glass, it always fell to us to sweep them up. Now-or-Laters. Snoopy, the second in a cavalcade of pets, would parade regally about the screened-in back porch. Daddy soaked then bathed him in a pan of gasoline to strip his coat of mange, so that when we spoke of him at all, it was as "under quarantine." Children often see with a clarity that adults ignore. Around the corner, down the hill, three blocks or so, until the fields of St. Catherine Labouré unreeled before us, as in the scenes in that movie usually broadcast during the "sweeps" preceding Christmas, the projector that lighted up the cinema of our childhood dreams. Desire is, among other things, a function of repetition, or so the very patterns of your life have led you to believe. No better place existed to fly kites or box-crates, except Penrose Park, where, one supposed, the nuns never chanced to set habit. You assembled the frame and tail according to the package's confusing directions, which required more than the recommended ten minutes. Junie aided him in getting his aloft, before it tangled and then plummeted with the others. The genius lies in the execution. The Ville, whose village. Shivering, you stood on the sunlight's skirt, yet they laughed as they looked right through you. Shrieks of all sizes and colors would distort the evening air, rendering it opaque and virtually unreadable. Who would not beg to stay out past curfew, when the excitement usually began. "Catch the ball, boy, catch the ball!" as it rearranged the contours of our face. "Tag" became the game of choice, though we occasionally improvised with "Batman" or with "Jonny Quest." Against form. Before the final closing of eyes and the "good night's sleep," the irrepressible march of twilight.

A Chain of Incidents, Antecedents, the Very Events Themselves

Memory, that vast orchard of myriad, variegated moments, appears to undergo an endless replanting. In the summer the heat would troll across the city like an immense seine, gathering every living and inanimate thing in its folds. This entails no notion of the "subject." Being of Southern blood, nearly all of them could bear it, though not without some cavils and some grudging. Chatillon-DeMenil. Ardor, or another, made the man next door shoot his wife, though at

ANNOTATIONS

[handwritten margin note: "which generation benefited most"]

the beginning there was little violence and still the white flight had begun. Contingency spells the death of certitude. Of course everyone had relatives in Arkansas and Mississippi who were on their way, since Negroes just two years before had finally won jobs at the Jefferson Bank. The impact of this pebble of history is barely felt nowadays, particularly by the generation that has benefited most. From West Florissant one could quickly reach the highway heading south to the riverfront, where the Arch and the riverboats reveled. Mill Creek Valley. Few of the homes had central air, a fact made obvious by a simple street review, as almost every other window distended with those plastic, wheezing boxes. This note: Baden sat less than a half-hour's walk away. Somnambulant majority. Like his mother he was said to possess a "viper's tongue," a trait leaving all but the older teachers wary. Her family had washed north in several tides, the main ebbing occurring shortly after the First World War. Whether they came by train or by carriage bears important historical implications. Aos pés da cruz. By his time several of the city's schools had been integrated, but the decisive court order lay decades away, and then how often would his parents repeat to him that Sumner High School, founded in 1875, was the "first comprehensive Black high school this side of the Mississippi." St. Louis was spared the riots of that era, despite the anger burgeoning in the projects. Many of the protesters lived within a few miles of where the slaves had been manumitted, a fact particularly evident in Wellston. Well, you needn't. Please print on the dotted line. This, as does each of these flares of intellection, takes note of the structural aspects of signification. Uncle Clarence and Aunt Emma stood guard before an armory of toys, a few of which were older than the century. Like most of the father's family, they represented a higher social class and the products of vibrant miscegenation. Years before, someone, in a spirit one might now term enterprising, had sold the family farm in St. Charles that would have been their birthright. Portage des Sioux. You spoke up, as was usual, but they simply chose to ignore you, interested instead in their game of spades, with its rising, idle chatter. The kitchen of his body in which the fires of history were blazing. In the sword tree there were Osage whom we mistook for Cherokees, which seemed not an uncommon occurrence. Certain actions need no convincing. Veronica, who could tell better stories than one might find in library books, thus assumed the role of playmommy, teaching you how to sing and fight and whom to call "meshugenah." Out of earshot, one heard talk of depression, accompanied by the occasionally unsubtle comment on her weight. Loneliness is solitude unfulfilled by its own presence. Their eyes fled this text, or perhaps its context, one infers, out of a fear of contamination. Mild and muddy springs, hot and humid summers, brief and balmy autumns, how they sabotaged one's readiness for winter. We were admonished to wear caps to prevent an attack of heatstroke, since our heads, small lots of blacktop, proved extraordinary attractors of sun. Ring-A-Levio. Still, he grew dizzy and dropped to his bed of sedge, which they dismissed as so much unnecessary drama. White reflects, relax. "Speak when you are spoken to and tuck in your lower lip, and save a big kiss for Maman," which each, like well-reared little boys, would have done without the threat of a "whupping." Night, a knowing not. Then you noticed the motorboat moored in the Deans' backyard, and went home and dreamt that someone might eventually sail her. The thought alone is often worth the promise. Perhaps out near Lake St. Louis, or in Illinois on Lake Carlyle, or more likely on the Missouri or the Lake of the Ozarks, though the important point was that they could at least afford to. Religion then was but one current in the river of our lives. Poinciana. By adolescence, most of these reflections had lost their color, which adulthood later restored from its dull and pallid palette.

Language, Knowledge, a Teeming River of Implications

A small yet insubordinate squadron of impressions had laid siege to his consciousness since infancy. Everything reposed beneath a glaze of dew, which was each morning's way of announcing its arrival. The slow greening of the daylight through the shutter slats, or evening, when the gangway grew sullen with darkness. Chances are. Shadows appeared to creep across the floor, until you focused to discover them ants. Photographs will substitute for a fully-sketched description. Waterbugs and spiders were really more common, rappelling down the tiles like mountaineers. In the jar, the aphids asphyxiated. With a view to pleasing the adults, you told no one. Moreover he could claim two godfathers, to everyone's amusement, of whom one had served quite honorably in Vietnam. The violent tenor of the recollections, perhaps resulting from a delayed effect, far exceeded what everyone had expected. Your tongue, but a bat in its cavern of reassurance, would take flight when you least expected it. Montgomery, My Lai. Many of the children, except those whose parents were considered "strivers," would walk to the neighborhood school. They first launched his punt at a Montessori Academy, which was thought to enhance a youngster's chances in life. There we could play with Legos of innumerable colors, a pint-sized oven that actually baked, and the other kids, including Patty, who soon became enamored of the red-haired boy. This was before one gained a sense of the "body" and could picture oneself "in affliction." Double talk. Eventually they took turns reading the "Negro" poets from those yellow-papered books whose covers had long ago disappeared. Usually we would sit and talk, or watch the TV set, or on warmer evenings walk several blocks with the dogs or alone for a "breath of fresh night air." Nice work, if you can get it, and you might get it if you lie. At the corner store, nickel candy and a sody pop, but only if you had been sterling. There never was, consequently, any incentive to steal, since this course of action had not been fostered alongside some greater moral lassitude. Pilfer, for a pal. Occasionally we heard shooting, but most often it was shouting, which a battle of fists or blades would readily resolve. <u>Our ears hammer impressions into audible jewels.</u> Further down the boulevard sat the unimposing branch library, further still the artist's studio. His wife, an artist in her own right, had sculpted the papier-mâché painting of Kali, which hung for years like a totem above the sofas. Chain of Rocks. You drew not only numerous studies of people, but a series of scenes to accompany them, yet they still denied that a child was capable of such work, convinced instead that you had traced or forged. Treemonisha. Just as well, heedlessness or laughter, a sure forgetting. The subsequent art teacher showed a mastery of the art of drawing lips and eyes, and thus encouraged us all to indulge in more identifiably "African" forms. Use a pen or pencil and answer all questions. A simpler example: a V with a circle on top, or a colorless ice-cream cone. Eugene Field House. Few things compared to culling lightning bugs live, since your mason jar theater became their nightstage. Roaches formed a different category altogether, like the stains that created a rusty crust upon the motel sheets, or that car that leapt the curb to cut the corner. "Em, eye, crookaletta, crookaletta, eye, crookaletta, crookaletta, eye, humpback, humpback, eye," and thus one could always avoid utter embarrassment in any blackboard bee. The result, a fathoming beneath the flourish of so many notes, a veritable exigesis. Music is the obvious analogue, that inimitable California poet tells us, which, in the context of the life that you have lived so far, is as much truth as trope. Yes and no. Yet, whenever the ice-cream truck would come by, the first impulse was to run to the window and perform the dance of seven wails. Who would not relent, before such shameless displays of talent. These episodes ceased, however temporarily, in the presence of "company," and at the family reunions, when all small ones were expected to be on their "absolute best behavior." Eventually the blight of crime and drugs would subsume the entire area, forcing a capitulation to the prerogatives of personal safety. And so, as his cousin said more eloquently than the mayor and the experts, when officials speak of "Urban Renewal," it's the Black folks that got to go.

ARRIVED AT BY R̲I̲T̲E̲S̲, BY R̲I̲T̲U̲A̲L̲S̲, A FINAL LINE OF DEFENSE

(handwritten annotation: against what, who)

In that house then, on that morning, as many in those families were Catholics, they were observed to interact in rhythms common to their faith and class, leaving abstract yet indelible imprints on the etching-plate of others. There who could ever truly "be a boy," given the demands of such games of truth. Magnificat. The grandparents' church sat on a street named Cote Brilliante, where the shade stood as still as the spire. They had become Presbyterians, a sect commensurate with a certain social standing. This preoccupation with the religious aspect points to a fuzzy, metaphysical nature. Natural Bridge. Several liquor stores sat in walking distance of that narrow, Negro crossroads, having reared and raised the men who owned them. Oh now, go to it, jazzmen. The excommunicated, like the divorced, were denied the most blessed sacrament, yet we refrained from overt comment on them as we had learned our contempt to be un-Christian. The paralyzing force of such inflexibility soon endeared you to certain Protestants, which only the testimony of succeeding years demonstrated the power to dispel. Underlining this were nuns who bore the names of exalted men, who taught their lessons in frowns and furrowed chins. In the end this disquieting descent left each child more unsure than before. His heart is a grotto bearing witness to others' kindnesses. A sudden musicality of phrase, as when one hears the windowpanes humming. Louis the Conqueror, not High John. Although in our sepia book of saints we were usually drawn to the visage of St. Martin de Porres, our city had received its name from the patron saint of France. Pronounced phonetically, after the British fashion. Religion now plays such an ambiguous role in American children's development. "Pass the plate, don't keep us late," which confirmed that he had originally been a Baptist. The priest, whose voice engraved these messages into our callow youth, would homilize before leading the whole congregration in song. Though his claps seldom managed to keep the beat, we thought them to be heartfelt. Nave of doves. A stranger terror lurked within the confessional,

transition

which was unlighted and reeked of sweat. Dance of the infidels. Aleikam salaam one replied to the man who peddled oils, incense, revolutionary tracts, and slender, mimeographed volumes of poetry. And so by the end of the Detroit riots they had chosen completely new names, thereby casting off another aspect of their heritage. Isis, Icarus, Iscariot, Idris. "I discovered that I could never remember how my favorite songs went," she wrote as if in anticipation of your "problem." Sunday-school lessons and softly spoken psalms had lodged in that crystalline realm of the mind which the swirl of adolescence would dissolve. To reach the building on Kingshighway required a half-hour drive from home, yet you could always sneak in through the side doors if late or you forgot your tithe, or beg for doughnuts if the culprits were gas and cigarettes. Something, however, points to behavior that is indisputably trifling. In the interim he flipped through the bulletins, which were troves of vital information. Memories, like cataracts, sometimes blind us to the present. All the cats come in. He prayed, kneeling solemnly on the rug's sandpapery surface, but his prayers remained wholly unanswered. A call, as always, upon the authority of the ancestors, at a pitch such as might befit a cantilene. Innumerable the issues they hid before the children, thinking them simply incapable of coping. Cousins who were Jehovahs argued that Jesus died on a tree, enlisting anecdotes and apocrypha as their proof. At Mass no one caught the spirit like those "Pennycostals" do. More baffling was why they called the holy bread the "host," why it could not touch our hands, and why it resided hidden in the "sepulcher."

[handwritten: trans]

Would it melt in the mouth or turn to flesh again, and then how on God's earth could someone swallow? Dim body, dazzling body. When the fun began it was frequently bedtime. Volubility unchecked in an imaginative child is a sure prescription for disaster. Although he tried to cloak these comments in a voiceless whisper, his voice dispersed the silence like a well-cast stone.

Texts, Context, a Fear of Contamination

Education, they counseled us, is the one, true key, yet the school was known less for its floors of tidy classrooms than for its gym with collapsible bleachers and that polished, hardwood floor. Promise-harness. The committee, comprising the clergy and the most prominent lay members, rechristened the complex after the first Black Catholic bishop, which provided even the most taciturn with an engaging topic of discussion. Simply naming, while powerful, never proves enough. He was usually charily chosen for the kickball teams, or last for any sport requiring aggression. A palpable terror, a shortness of breath. Consolation lay in the reading contests and the sketching assignments, when we could excel far beyond the expectations of both teachers and friends. My teeth cast a gleaming net for you, a white and wordless reply. Cardinal Ritter. "Poetry" served then as the recitative of bible-men and the pimp who stayed on the corner, or the huckster who with brio sold them a faulty vacuum cleaner. In those days we could recall the names and life stories of the major Black inventors almost as readily as our multiplication tables, though in truth a disjuncture persisted between their paradigms and how we perceived them, which neither teachers nor other adults sought to bridge. No one really slept at naptime. After the wedding, marked by a holy sacrament which he believed he understood, he and the other children brought Mrs. Orange her namesake fruit. In fourth grade, following a premise that defied "equality," the classes cleaved into two distinct and ability-based homerooms, which garnered for the smaller, brighter class a rancor it little deserved. "Freedom School." Thus that year proceeded by way of experimental groupings and methods, which sound nothing short of radical in the context of education today. Many the nuns who scored the names of saintly men in their heads until each was resurrected by reflex, and who, in daily sweeps past their desks, left a near-visible trail of camphor. With your hair cut so short, the older boys renamed you "Shine," rubbing your head as though it were their own personal talisman.

"Sensitive." Yet who did not desire to follow their model, for they were more real than his idols. What little boys do. Behavior enough to gain us mention in the newspaper, where he spoke of his desire to be popular, or in the parlance of those days, the "Caped Crusader." Ivanhoe, Pip, and Peter Pan led the list of childhood favorites, though it was hard to identify with that bespectacled, British "John." His father would not hesitate to mine him for that single ore of truth, since this, he had convinced himself, was a father's chief occupation. If you therefore were one who regularly lied, then your recollections might consist of the sum total of your childhood fictions. He waited but the invitations never materialized, so he learned to create small diversions for himself. A cleansing thus ensued, an art of remembering developed, a renewal undeniably the result. "Straight-A, Straight-A, nothing but a sissyboy who's scared to play," they screamed burning tracks across the playground, their faces brown, blazing globes of glee, as he crumpled near the swingset like a raveling, forgotten husk-doll. Repression's effects assume manifold forms. One option proposed seriously was that of skipping a grade, though they feared that might warp her emotional development. In other words, neither parent had expected such a fragile character, though they bore the verdict better once they had bought it. Some children are badly suited to this world, though their elders rarely gather this fact until the dawn of the teen years, when the complement of options has shrunk to zero. Baldwins reclined between a Jong, several Cozzenses, and two Morrisons, but Michener's opera had long held sway of the bookshelf. Neither Bolivia nor Paraguay has an ocean port, you learned from encyclopedias at the great-aunt's house. A few of them so old that they crumbled between the fingers, others crinkled with that odor of never having been fully opened. The genius lay in the execution, or at least in how she kept the deception from becoming apparent. Ebony and Black Enterprise graced the marble coffee table, though Jet garnered everyone's initial review. Our generation possesses only a cursory sense of the world that our ancestors braved, though the burdens of history bear unmovably upon us. Homer G. Phillips. Rollerskating in the summer around Steinberg Rink, or else in one of many indoor halls, and when he was old enough to wield a racket, tennis in O'Fallon Park. Sugarloaf Mound. One assessment: the chill cast the courts in a crepuscular light. Stan, who coached the older, lither players, sported a thick, beguiling mustache, while coiled hairs spilled from the V-neck of his jersey, leaving us with a sensation that we were yet unable to name. Ruby, my dear. "Swing, baby, lemme hear that ball sing and dance, serve, but not so much racket string, you got it, now, whoa, don't fling it." By perfecting a strategy, we learned gradually, we could organize and master almost any game, a lesson as applicable and valuable outside the court as on it.

II

IN THE FACE OF THE NIGHT'S HYSTERIA, WE SHOULD LIKE
TO POINT OUT, QUIETLY, THAT WHATEVER HAPPENED
IS EXPLICABLE.
Samuel R. Delany

AFTER ALL, IT WAS ONLY OUR
LIFE, OUR LIFE AND ITS FORGETTING.
Li-Young Lee

FOR IN THE BILLOWING AIR I WAS FLEET AND GREEN
RIDING BLACKLY THROUGH THE ETHEREAL NIGHT
TOWARDS MEN'S WORDS WHICH I GRACEFULLY UNDERSTOOD
Frank O'Hara

CLEANSING, THROUGH THE ART OF REMEMBERING, A RENEWAL

Picnics swarmed those summers as fervidly as bees, though he feigned to ignore the insects unless they graced him with a sting. Wasps and garter snakes composed a different cohort, sending you screaming through the screen door in out of the dark. "La Ba-Kair." Certain sensations are unrenderable in sequential terms. Even small animals recognize this. To salve a yellowjacket attack his mother would apply baking soda. In essence she was redrawing the outer surface of his "lovemap." Towards the end of May the city would parade its wares before the river like a tired, forsaken bride. This entails a "localized" notion of the subject. The two aunts, which is what we also called close female family friends, resided in the Laclede Town Houses, where Damie used to keep her beauty shop. Whether these still present advisable housing options no longer remains in doubt. Analysis involves a subtler mode of seeing. Chestnut Valley Sound. It was assumed that they would eventually own property like the TV families, though no one had taken much account of the difficulties involved in obtaining a mortgage. By then the flow of white residents away had become a hemorrhage but there was almost still no de facto desegregation. William Greenleaf Eliot. During the weeks leading up to the Fourth of July, they drove all day to Grand Rapids, where he imagined the ground wore a purple shawl of lilacs and the legions of "cousins" would greet us as though we were returning from exile. There, the earth lay parched and bare, though you remember more the orderly grid of streets. The trellis of names of his grandfather's people climbed bewilderingly before him, thus he reconstructed each cousin's relation on a daily basis. A Golden Gloves boxer, an amateur star. Who knew what to make of the other grandmother's people, whose aloofness one took for granted. Vain vacuity. At first he would squirm in the barber's chair, lest they inflict on him another Quo Vadis, but as he aged he learned to appreciate the barber's focused attention, the tender, careful play of those fingers. "Tutti-frutti, good bootie," Afro-Sheen, Congo Queen. The coolest picks, plastic, tricolored, with long metal prongs, flaunted their power-fist end first, and because they could not stay corralled in a pocket, one had to be vigilant so as not to lose them. Upright in our afros like coxcombs brought dismay to the faces of our mothers, but how else could we boys display them so that the girls would not fail to see them. "Well, how do I look?" knowing that no one with any decency would answer. The desire to be seen was an attempt to escape alterity, or in other words, to shift from the margins to the center. If he has to then he ought to, but he needn't. One learned not to slam the oven door since the cake inside might fall, and to wash one's hands with vigor before sitting down at table. Then the father would order a pizza since he could not cook, though by seven Jeffrey, the younger brother, had become handy with flapjacks. The effect is essentially novelistic, though its fictiveness remains another matter. Summer itself was often not a strong enough attractor, so they adorned it with a garland of festivals. At the Veiled Prophet Fair, or the Strassenfest, which was smaller, couples traded leers and melodies while waltzing about the grounds in lederhosen. One is often prone to reduce such situations to the results of lifestyle choices. Through the air interlaced the aroma of wurst and sauerkraut with almost visible ribbons of beer, Raus, Ihr kleine Mäuser, raus. Juneteenth, later, crowning the most torrid month, when the scions of the former slaves celebrated their ongoing battle for freedom. Inquiry thereby becomes a ceaseless aspect of living, its complement a vital and vigorous sense of improvisation. Against meaning. Lacking any concept of the "body" beyond its being the locus of received sensations, his self-esteem derived mainly from what others identified in him physiquely. In your case your hair was never considered completely "good," which was why she quickly picked your friend instead. Imagine: one's fingers as the branches from which the fruits of one's desires tumble. You hid but they had quit the game some hours before, thus in the end no one came seeking. The problem is one of choosing. Daddy was always eager to play catch, since he felt society expected this from a loving, caring father. A confidence that soared and a glovehand that fell, still there was no baseball near either. Duplicity has killed more Black men than gin. In a southpaw, what they appreciate most is this sort of "live arm." From his mouth words rushed like richly fed rapids, leaving him ever vulnerable to ascription.

Records, Accounts, Accumulation as Explication

The sun rose and the sun set yet he did not leave the bed. Eventually you would come to rationalize these events as minor flaws of character. A clue, alcohol. Blue barge of our sympathies, float past this scene of woe. Melodrama substituted for melancholy. Holidays, folks buzzed and flitted about like fruit flies, yet as a child you lacked the power to shoo them. Inevitably epithets would detonate upon the driveway's head or a fist would soar through the air to its punch, but we grinned as if suspended, gay lanterns through the outplaying of each episode, for we realized only twilight could ensure a dimming of the hubbub. Absent of all of these kernels of drama those occasions might have proven less festive, although the bitter winter months would have departed sooner. [Easter, that Christian estuary.] Caps, scarves, and Afros bloomed upon their heads like versicolored, April crocuses. We took pride in showing off our newly made suits, which testified to our grandmother's artistry. Old shoes with their patina of brown polish, old socks where the heels had worn threadbare. The photographs document the changes in the family's sense of fashion, but reveal no more than a hint of the unraveling of its internal social fabric. Creditors calling night and day. Complain, and you might be blamed. On Thanksgiving after Nana had cleared the turkey and dressing and the turnip greens from the dining-room table, everyone would gather to play Po-Ke-No. The grown folks gossiped and argued over bid-whist or poker while we huddled before the prime-time specials. "Whatever you do, don't touch the cards in the kitty," a command that they learned to obey. No niggers, renegers. The reviled and unschooled "Mississippi" types. Perhaps there are exaggerations that enhance the flow of a few of these stories, but each, on the whole, constitutes a regime of truth. Fleur-de-lys. Needless to repeat, someone kept saying that the troops were coming home, though the news commentator's words contradicted this. A disproportionate number from that neighborhood, crippled in combat. One still identified with him and wanted him too.

If the number of your dependent children has increased during the weeks claimed, you must report to your local office to claim the dependency allowance. Around that time they found lead in the wallpaper. Maudlin malingerers, lingering madly. Consider: images of Vietnam, the assassinations, and Watergate bear that fuzzy, bluish-white glimmer, since nearly all your recollections of that era's major events are but the residue of each evening's televised diversions. Despite the activism the uneven terrain of history remains, the challenge, however, no longer to write the unrecorded story. What's going on. The Vanderfords, meaning Big Preston and Cleo, kept a pen full of beagles, "the hunting dogs," which were loosed in that collision with the trailer. Marion, sleeping at the time like a cat in sunlight, did not even suffer a concussion. Accidents, like epiphanies, deplete one's store of metaphors. Pannonica. "Don't think you're getting away with something, 'cause I know you better than you know yourself," so how were we, mere children, to respond. However, they polished off a jug of Koolaid by themselves and lay sick to their stomachs during dinnertime. In other words, innocence, no sense, a nuisance. Blindslight rendered the story that he was beginning unreadable, thus he settled for staging wars between his miniature militias. One's back is the stairwell to the attic of one's thoughts, or the pilaster shoring up one's shoulder-eaves. And so in her elaborate mythology of action, if it was not uncouth it was unorthodox, and if not unorthodox, obnoxious, and if it did not fit within this carefully constructed rubric, then it simply was not worthy of expression. Given this as your premise, you were lucky to continue down the path of literature at all. Turner Hall Turnverein. And so, encased in each attempt to make himself heard lies the aim to site his personal development within the broader historical record.

*trans
St. louis based
German gymnyst
(32)*

SIGNS, SCENES, A PSYCHIC TRAIL OF ASSIGNATIONS

Sex, that sublime sum of bodily attraction, served as little more than one factor in the algebra of their juncture. Would they kiss, as they were expected to, or go further, as their parents hoped and feared. Chances are. Yet the light and the hours spun out to their end like spindles spinning free of thread. At the party, given to introduce him to manhood, his hips turned with Peggy's like finely tuned gears. She was thirty, he fourteen. Lion of the Valley. Guilt hung around his neck like an asafetida bag, warding off all but the most persistent fantasies. "Don't be bringing no babies into this house," uttered as much to persuade as to warn. They seemed incapable of conceiving of gay or lesbian people, except in terms of slurs or epithets. A word is a sword that cuts with less effort, though the wounds will often last longer. The man in the hat and trenchcoat approached him in a way that was not considered quite acceptable. A sly glance, espied, from the corners of the eyes. Shame, and more of the same. Oppression is most effective when its aims are effected voluntarily. The one or two girls that you raised the courage to call wanted more than anything to be considered best friends. Still one dreamt up schemes to enter that schema, which conferred on its residents the validation of "normality." She giggled, then inched towards the passenger-side door when your hand flopped fish-flat onto her thigh. Primitive parameters. Intuition provided the first step, information the second, until he realized that by combining the two he was creating a handy index of being. We were always the first to grace the dance floor, for our self-esteem derived primarily from others initially identified in us physiquely. Evonce. Boys should not flap their arms when they run downstairs, or cover their mouths when they laugh. Dignity is occasionally a byproduct of discretion. Let's get it on. By focusing on his footwork, he could think of the men he had spotted on the street and still not lose his rhythm. Meanwhile, her shawl slid down unhurriedly, to reveal lightly lotioned, amber shoulders. Who had no idea of how to meet another, or how to love another, and this was before our current plague era [AIDS]. Things were rumored to occur in "The Loop" in Forest Park, where the curtain of trees kept most actions hidden. One need not overlook the beauty cast by a man's hands, though as with women the face and lower regions usually garner the most attention. "Watch your date and not the other guys dancing," he chimed to himself as reinforcement. Reality, that rude intruder. After the fingers reached the chest and the legs locked, everything proceeded much more smoothly. A soothing stroke. Your penis is a woodwind that some play better than others. What two men do. He sang but they hardly listened and so they could not repeat what they had heard. "Who can make head or tail of these so-called stories," as if this were not the aim of your [accusing] aesthetic. The fundamental instability of two lovers' relationship becomes most apparent when they must live together, since cohabitation tends to magnify the sharpest edges of any personality. Avoid contact with magnetic surfaces. Of course we knew the general proscriptions for comportment, but being teenagers frequently failed to follow them, imagining ourselves nearly men, on the adult side of twenty-one. Fun after dark, though of the sort best enjoyed by one alone. Later that night their fingers passed from the Ouija board to each other's shoulders, thighs, yet not one rose to flee the room or uttered a single cry. Accusations flew, but we knew. Straight, no chaser. Though effective as an initial strategy, transgression devolves swiftly into an end in itself.

[marginalia: exactly / not / progress]

A Fathoming Beneath a Flourish of Notes, an Exigesis

Desire, among other things, derives its force from repetition, or so your general pattern of behavior would lead you to believe. Neither parent had initially expected such a fragile character, though they hid their disappointment beneath a flurry of activity. Ut natura poesis: autumn arrived to our wonderment, introduced by the river's murmur. Stands of birches, poplars, shuddered with delight, as the park glimmered with the embers of Indian summer. Carondelet. His hopes and dreams were maturing with each subtle change in the weather, like the peppers she had suspended from the gaspipe. Ambivalence towards the cool and fleeting day, towards the cold and stolid night hours. Play your number. Your mother was extraordinarily attentive to gradations of demeanor, which allowed her to catalogue, to cope with, the frequent shifts in attitude. Comprehension does not hinge upon an image. The view beyond the patio too was transforming as through a kaleidoscope, changing daily its array of moods and colors into ever more awe-provoking patterns. Our dreams are but hulls for our souls. Every house had a dog, but only one dog had a doghouse. We would leap upon the car hoods when a mad dog came charging, or failing this we shimmied up the telephone poles. The authority inherent in each of these words never exceeds the dictates of practical truth. Then they would put on the albums or forty-fives and dim the basement lights, and begin to perform the newest dance. Such delivery, a diva. Everyone studied their moves with care so that at someone else's house they would not slip up. In this way, a sense of tradition was nurtured, which others wrongly attributed to their "nature." He was afraid of standing with his back to the curb, for fear that the unknown might seize him. "Scaredy-cat, scaredy-cat, too scared to know where your shadow's at!" After a certain age it was not considered proper to sew, just as it had never been appropriate to knit, and yet in late adolescence and adulthood he would require these skills, as well as the ability to darn. The cooler boys built their own go-carts, while the wealthier ones received scooters or velos, but for him a bicycle would have to suffice, even though it devoured his mother's entire paycheck. With glee they assembled the roadster, the chief pleasure coming from the effects of the glue. Bakai. Brief observation of any personality proves that human existence cannot be reduced to a science. "Fat meat is greasy, dark meat is sweet," which always induced a burst of laughter, since they were expecting what they had been promised, a few lines from an Augustan. By choosing and extolling certain models to the exclusion of all others, he sought to deny the impending crisis of his own self-representation. Beneath the brownblack thicket of your hair a trove of information lies waiting. Then they remembered how, after supper, their parents had read to them slowly, which taught them to appreciate the aural potency of words. Analysis entails a subtler mode of seeing. The concatenation of names rose like a conjurer's prologue: Brazil, Liberia, Nigeria, Cuba, Eritrea. Silence poses a unique dilemma. Language leads to one bank, knowledge to the other, yet little prepares them for fording the teeming river of expectations. Who would say "bed" when "grave" was more accurate, who denied a distinction between "naming" and "calling." Yet a great fear inheres in much of what was discussed, for something points to behavior that was "trifling." The dyspeptic Confederate doctor, however, consequently wanted no part of his son, and so he named him after the demoted Union general before abandoning him altogether. Later the mythology would fulfill itself, creating a whole new myth of their paternal origins. Soulard Market. Of course she was overjoyed that she could pass as a Filipino or when tanned as a product of some "Caribbean island's gentry," a fact which they derided with snide remarks, though they secretly envied her "passport." In D.C. or Atlanta is where you'll find a real landed Black society, he recalled his father preaching, in scorn of the rivertown's provincial elite. "And don't you get no airs cause ain't nobody stuttin' you," advice so sound that whosoever could might risk denying it. The threat and the promise, Palmares. Our generation lacks more than a cursory sense of the world that our ancestors faced, which surprises no one cognizant of the contempt in which the nuances of history are currently held. The function and effect of titles, as in most cases of naming, however, depends on one's ability to differentiate signs. Ornithology. And so, in an effort to make so many shorter stories richer, these overtures ought to be read as a series of extended annotations.

The Territory of History, Whose Unrecorded Story

Toynbee, in a letter to the prior, his friend and spiritual advisor, proposed the thesis that St. Louis had consisted of an originary Creole core. This center, he argued, successive waves of English Southerners and Yankees, then Irish, and later Germans, had subsumed, thereby eliding the reality of the pre-Spanish Indian presence or the various African slaves and freemen who had helped to found the city in 1764. Men are the question, and their efficient reintegration.

Jacques Clamorgan. Such was the splendor of those erstwhile eras, when the streetcars ran from St. Charles to Kirkwood. Slaves had been sold at market on the steps of the grand courthouse that we now glided through in awe. The tour guide, however, slighted this aspect of the building's history, believing this subject disruptive and unrelated to his evocations. Steerage, so as to get over here. Who spoke of the African-American denizens, through the metaphor of an unablatable excrescence. Chauffeur's Club combos. A nearly incestuous series of interrelations allowed the founding families to retain their property and titles. Pierre de Laclède de Liguest. Some forty years later the gynecomastic general approved the fire sale as a way of cutting his losses, though great doubt remains in many minds as to whether the land was his to sell. To what extent is American history the history of American capital. But that former Haitian slave wrought all of this. If they could only have steered him to the piano sooner, he might have elected a more worthwhile enterprise. So much of our sense of identity depends on this desire for attention, yet we conversely deem it unseemly to draw great notice to ourselves. Incongruous, in Congress. Later the laity repainted the walls so that the saints resembled their families. As in all propaganda, substance was sacrificed for superficial appeal. We took turns reciting the "Negro" poets at one of those gatherings for children that bourgeois yet working-class parents felt would instill a sense of pride and self-recognition. These occasions, arrived at by appropriating known and invented rituals, constituted, as they would eventually comprehend, a fragile line of defense. By the end of two years most of the families had dropped out, proving that indifference constitutes a political stance too. It is better not to mention names as they often indict the collective memory. If in doubt refer to the operation manual. Dumas School. Some of those formerly "colored" institutions would eventually vanish through consolidation as part of the desegregational restructuring plan, their memories blazons on the minds of their alumni, their names empty vessels of sound to the children who might roam their abandoned grounds today. The effect, from this coign of vantage, verges plainly on the novelistic. But oh, Saint Louis, such a colored town, a minefield of myth and memory. Their father, while listening to Coltrane, was poring through Cleaver in the evenings, though it would be a few years before they connected that author with the pig-eared copy of Soul on Ice. Ron Karenga, another. Daddy also coached basketball as a means of providing those boys with a viable life-alternative. Later on, he was as prone to drink as he was to cuss, a fact that rapidly trained them to tread as if on crystal. Note that it is easy to underestimate the power of representation, and yet to fixate on this site of contestation to the exclusion of other problematic areas is to consign the nature of the struggle to the scopopsychic realm. Uh-huh. With the tape recorder she fashioned her own call-in program, devoted to the theme of history, which allowed her to bypass the usual crank callers and the necessity of masking her voice. "And what on earth are we supposed to do with you now," to which you balked at furnishing an answer. As the child of an alcoholic one tends to retreat from conflict, which engenders further conflict itself. Transforming the letters, nevertheless, into fully formed words was as important a confidence-builder as keeping the bike aloft on the graveled road or reaching the lake's mile marker. Thus he wrote but they professed to comprehend not a word, claiming the entire text unfolded like a riddle. Black pearls. The doctor, a born-again Christian, approached his mother in a way that was not quite acceptable, which he couched within a discourse of "friendship" and "salvation." In retrospect you see why others failed to intervene, though at the time this marked the final betrayal. One's trunk thus brimmed with daggers of vengeance, which one sheathed to forestall any bloodshed. In all of this we detect the influence of the media, which points to a fundamental failure of resistance. Kinds of blue. Truth, that abstruse and unrepenting philosopher wrote, is another aspect of revealing.

A Call to the Ancestors, a Cantilene

With each move we refashioned fresh and functional identities, imposed in part by the will of each new neighborhood's children, influenced too in part by these opportunities to be reborn. The prisonhouse of cogito. Scenarios: alternately Friday and Crusoe, at other points Gallant or Goofus, most often one of the numerous TV characters like J.J. or Fonzie or Raj, but then there appeared that moment at the peak of yet another family crisis when he proclaimed himself the next Percy Shelley. They consequently decried literature as a guide to the life that one lived, as mere retreat, fool's flight from the world's true horrors, but instead he derived from these stories, those poems, maps to realizable liberty, and took in each finished text a step ever closer to the zone of deliverance. East Saint Louis. In Los Angeles and its environs, scale appeared to warp itself, for they drove and they drove and they drove some more, yet they still had not gotten there. What he noticed first were the palm trees hovering above, the heat's white shuddering at the horizon, the waves' soft churning as they lapped upon the shore, the sparkling mazes of the supermarkets. Out of earshot, shouts and whispers. So much to tell which they concealed from the children, convinced of their inability to cope. One's mouth is the runway from which the possible taxis, alights in words, or the hangar in which life's verities, lies lie dormant. Left alone you marched through all of the Dr. Seusses, then shocked them by declaiming passages aloud. "Keep reading in this dim light, you're gonna lose your eyesight," a warning unheeded before the promise of so much prose. We could spend hours in the upstairs stacks just wiping dust from the spines in order to examine the titles better. Who recited the four main rivers that feed the Missouri in Missouri—the Gasconade, the Osage, the Locust, the Chariton—though the Cuivre River flows into the Mississippi. Your memory is transformative as opposed to eidetic, which best serves the purposes of literature or lying. Other times the jones they traded could have filled their own dictionary, which led him to indite a mini-lexicon. Klactoveededstene.

how close the innovation is to lying

composition by Dizzie Gillespie

And so we never, under any circumstances, experienced a dearth of interesting material, nor did we ever presume we might be wasting our time. Back at home, in the waters of the Northlands pool, he began his training to become a "dolphin," which the traumatic event at the Tiny Tots school would disastrously interrupt. She placed her heel on his best friend's head, daring either to cry or to climb out of the water. A terrible wailing, a scream from below. Myth or mendacity, depending on how you tell it. After the hurling into the deep end your confidence returned, so that as you swam for the bobbing buoy you considered only the mirthful aspect of that moment. Still, when one speaks of ethics one is implicitly speaking of actions, and when one talks of morals one is talking about beliefs. Poorly marked or unmarked responses will count against your total. Nana required that we bow our heads and utter a passage of Scripture before lifting even napkin or fork, while at home we rarely prayed, but simply plunged right in. The other grandmother, Maman, never obliged them to say grace, however manners mattered at her table too. "Clear the peas off your plate, please," achieved with the aim to appease. Raised on the harsh Mississippi soil, the grandfather knew the rudiments of self-sufficient farming, such as how to keep bugs from devouring potatoes without pesticides, or how to sow okra seed, and leading them down to the drainage lagoon, explained the lack of necessary acreage for corn. In their minds, as in the then-current television shows, however, the farmer still continued to constitute a mildly romantic figure. Federated Block Units. In such cases you might recur to therapy against the more infrequent response of analysis, just as one in a political setting might appeal to nature against interpretation. "Salt peanuts, salt peanuts," the President gaily sang, words the little boys knew belonged to Daddy and "Dizzy." Joplinesque. To speak of culture is to foreshadow a battle. And so when the fun began it was bedtime, few pleas for leeway proving persuasive. He fled as a matter of course but no one deigned to follow, so he eventually had to skulk back home. Giant steps. Love, therefore, assumes the status of a cynosure, when in truth it is but one outward manifestation of the internal discourse of returning.

III

BEHOLD ST. LOUIS, CITY HONORED NEAR AND FAR,
NAMESAKE OF THE GREAT CRUSADER,
IN COLUMBIA'S CROWN, A STAR!
Susan Louise Marsh

A LEADING CITIZEN WROTE IN 1818 THAT "THE PREVAILING
LANGUAGE OF THE WHITE PERSONS ON THE STREETS WAS FRENCH;
THE NEGROES OF THE TOWN SPOKE FRENCH. ALL THE INHABI-
TANTS USED FRENCH TO THE NEGROES,
THEIR HORSES, AND THEIR DOGS."
Audrey L. Olson

ST. LOUIS / SUCH A COLORED TOWN / A WHISKEY BLACK
SPACE OF HISTORY & NEIGHBORHOOD / FOREVER OURS TO
LAWRENCEVILLE
Ntozake Shange

Multeities, Disjunctions, Intense Polysemic Pleasures

By the autumn of his childhood they had abandoned their prefab in the ghetto for a ranch house in a suburb whose property values and lack of crime could boast of national renown. No one, you understand, carped at the size of the required down payment, since it was assumed that they would eventually own their own property. Ignorance is incapable of concealing itself. Out there many of the Blacks were descended from the slaves or servants who had once managed those estates, so tensions were bound to abound when the educational system finally integrated. Douglass School. Few Negro families had settled land as far out as Red Bud, though even Franklin and Jefferson Counties had shown a minimal Black presence since well before the Civil War. This unconcern with the questions of whether a "there" was there, or of what this "there" consisted, remained unnamed until a later encounter with what they were denouncing as "pragmatism." History has been kindest to the charming old German quarter, where the wealthier or more committed ones had hidden in their rathskellers those dark fugitives headed north for freedom. Information, he first noticed, in a series of notes that someone had inscribed in the narrow, running margin. "Missouri Compromise." Out there then one never needed to lock one's doors or speak to one's neighbors for weeks. Once a week a man, bearing more than a minor resemblance to the president whose name became a cussword, delivered orange juice and grape drink and lemonade just as they had observed in the movies. My address, Madras. Hush Puppies, bell-bottom denims, a Bengal-striped shirt, though you refused to be photographed in platforms. A fulvous swatch of velour that tired the eyes, your sweater was the only one lighter than your skin. "Dibs on your Tootsie-Roll" was all they had to say to quash any attempts to deny them, so you broke it into morsels as had been demonstrated on TV, and went home without anticipating a "Thank you." Boys should not flap their arms when they run down stairs, or cover their mouths when they laugh, proscriptions made less to correct a child's deportment choices than to allay a parent's useless fears. "Though the crust may be brown the bread is still white." Lacking any real conception of evil, a child is prone to explore the limits of her will. He fought back but they laughed at him, so that he discovered his skill as jokester, but he kept in mind the example of Richard Pryor. Mode for Joe. The father eventually began to dwell on the numerous half-veiled jealousies this move and its aftermath induced. Often, he would speak of Captain Wendell O. Pruitt, and the other Tuskegee flyers, who had never been properly honored. Just remembering the treatment of all those distinguished Black airmen filled his eyes with tears of awe and bitterness. Benign neglect. Who stood and saluted when the flag flapped high, who sang the anthem without anger. Time is no equalizer. As you will recall she was a blond divorcée with two attractive kids, whom she appeared to love more dearly than she did the thought of them. Although working-class and Irish, they quickly ignited a friendship, which differed from what we had encountered in the city. Civility offers an acceptable way to evade the issues at hand. Name us anonymous. "Grumio erat coquus," he yelled out in earnest, to the consternation of a number of his classmates and the instructor. Chalk hurled at the head was the usual punishment, though kneeling while hoisting a dictionary was not unknown. My mind is the sandbox that my thoughts play in, or the court in which they exercise their claims to reason. Nine, the magic number. Quietly they strode through the grounds of the Eden Seminary, the thrill of actually being there far more compelling than anything they encountered therein. Reinhold Niebuhr. Accordingly, along with the doctrinal classes the Opus-Dei brothers offered scale-model construction; however, journalism more thoroughly captured his mood. By then it was the Bicentennial, and you were playing "John Henry" in the program at the Loreto-Hilton, which entailed memorizing a medley of songs, and learning how to swing an invisible hammer. Hurry up this way again. More the name of the Algonquin Golf Club where one caddied than any other identifiable aspect, and the waiting buckets of crawdads which made the traipse across the greens go more quickly. Of course, the city's importance had diminished progressively since the days when it had served as the gateway to the West, though one's perspective on this fact waxes as one gains distance from it. DeSoto. Having abandoned it for the far more sterile suburbs, they were drawn back to that laboratory of human interaction. Against closure. As a result those endlessly engaged in the quest for happiness usually constitute the unhappiest lot. Anthropology offers us among its many conclusions that boys throw a certain way, girls another.

THESES, ANTITHESES, A WELTER OF THEORIES

Trundling through the pass of bald maples across the valley of ice, he felt bound irrevocably to the outside world and to some inner, still aspiring self. Schneeblick, so blink now. Daylight, reflecting off the soundless frostscape of the nursery, transformed his hands into two bars of franklinite. The early, wintry sunsets arrived, and then, although they waited, nothing. O soul, sublime subject of bodily subtraction, which the sky has entombed in all this whiteness. He cowered in fear of the implications of such thoughts, yet brazenly continued to think them. His mother nevertheless purchased two pairs of long johns which inevitably curled and shrank. These scaled the calves like spiders, forcing one to wrench until they reached the socks. Indifference is not the same as ambivalence, which proceeds from different situational premises. Joliet, Père Marquette. Most winters pinched the flesh like pincers, yet a few hacked through the bones like scythes. Often the ground glared back as would a freshly Windexed mirror, so that when he fell, breaking what the doctor termed a "coccyx," seven years of bad luck became part of the bargain. One loses 90 percent of one's body heat through the head, though most worry about the throat, feet, and limbs. "Where did you leave your gloves this time?" which kept us silent, praying against frostbite. Catch-a-girl, kiss-a-girl. One could still go tobogganing down the steeper part of Art Hill, but there were lesser hills much closer in the more historic parts of Webster, where the dauntless ones could sled or ski-board on a stolen trashcan top. On your back, in the snow, making angels the sun would summon. White swath. Summer they awaited for its bounty of trips and excursions, such as a return to Meramec Caverns or Silver Dollar City, now, from what he read, not far from where the Klan was presently headquartered. A cathode bath usually proves easier than self-immersion in a written text, thus did the ends of those evenings eddy through that small, transfixing screen. On the other hand, you noted at the Monet exhibit at the Art Institute of Chicago, which you attended with your classmates and the chaperone, that although painting had once served as the transcriptor of the soul, it now mainly served to break the hold of mechanical reproduction. The effect is essentially Suric, or "Quranic" with the subject matter secular. What seized their interest without parallel was the spectacle of the soldier grinding with the half-asleep young woman, which they watched through the undraped hotel window, while their elders snored two rooms away. Boys view, voyeurs. Yet he persisted in his interpretation of the surface of the oil, or was it charcoal mixed with oil, since for something so thick and black that one can make little of it, appreciation becomes an effect rather than an immediate feeling of the picture, followed by a gradual perceptive glowing. A guide, unbidden. Now he sings, now he sobs. And so although the choice between competingoptions creates a thicket of perplexing problems, one still can envision that open meadow of narrative possibilities, as that New York poet of the process of makes clear in his expressively opaque treatise. "Stop where you are and do not move," the policemen yelled out in unison. Dizzy, however, he dropped to his frozen, grassy bed, which they disdained as "so much unnecessary drama." I'n-Shta-Heh. Mittened, parkaed, he etched the scene around him with a penknife on a board the reverend had discarded. Please read directions carefully before opening. Stripped bare of all life, all color, the outdoors seemed in mourning, so we crept towards the road on our tiptoes, cringing that our crunching might offend. Lester leaps in. They too were unable, remember, to categorize to their satisfaction the book of drawings, and went about dismissing them as the products of a "troubled" mind. Snowblink, now blink, see. One's thoughts are the goads that drive one's calf-like existence forward, strange, diaphanous gods reappearing day and night. Marronage. Seen properly as a field of multeities, characterized by the presence of so many disjunctions, one might learn to appreciate this experience if only for the intense polysemic pleasures that it offers. Worry later. And so it was at that time when you lacked any real notion of the "body" that your grandfather lay silent on his deathbed, cradling you in his still strong arms. Appalled, they refuse to believe that you have told, since they remember your vows of silence.

Permanence or Evanescence, the Process of the Real

The studied obscurity of those avant la lettre poets derives primarily from their desire to conceal. In your eyes, however, she reckoned the plight of the artist, which seduced her even more thoroughly, though you protested rightly that such suffering pales in comparison to what most other human beings endure. Trumpet-in-the-morning. Then mother left for work as father was returning half-asleep from his shift, so bundled up we too set off along the longer route that passed the stately "Century" houses. Another path, across the train tracks near the home for "wayward girls," where he leered and poked his crotch through the fence, until the stones began to rain upon him. Recall how before you had spent the afternoons with Nana, and how when you grew old enough to walk to school your peculiar cast of companions, though your dispositions often left you all at war. Our legs are the pistons that fire our march through life, or at night two pipes through which each previous day's dramas drain. Circuits, circadia. The long way had led past Mr. Ward's gas station, where Gandy, known as "Sarge" from his army days, repaired cars. The other way promised a leaf-canopied stroll through a modest residential section, which you imagined had been the haunts of that playwright's "Toussaint," and the store not far from the abandoned trolley tracks, where one could linger over stalls of tangerines and Chinese apples or on hot days purchase taffy and "Bomb Pops." Comparing this much later to the daily drives out to the Priory in Crève Coeur, what strikes you most is how fundamental and relative the relations are between distance and perspective. Back-and-Forth. "What will it take to get this garden growing?" a clarion to lift the rake and hoe, though the result would remain that patch of scrub that cumbered in the shade of the collapsing carport. Through the window of the backporch where the great-aunt sheltered her orchids, one surveyed with admiration the bay of asters, zinneas, and marigolds, and by stretching one's senses just a quarter of a yard, one could almost touch the impatiens that cloaked the edges of the gangway.

Grandfather, on the other hand, cultivated several plots of fruits and vegetables, among them tomatoes, turnips, carrots, sweet potatoes, onions, and watermelons, which sated both mind and stomach, especially during the desperate years. A little work is a wondrous thing, too much toil becomes a torment. Consequently when they began to cook peas as well as plant, pick, and shell them, it clarified once and for all the formerly central role of agriculture. Therapy, and not analysis, is our normal mode of reaction. This interpretation, however, of the poet's striking originality failed to cite his filial reliance on preexisting discourse. By clever manipulation of a French accent, he convinced the teacher that he had lived in Martinique. She grimaced as you described fishing in São Paulo because she knew you were no longer just recounting but had crossed the lying-line. "Is that any way to behave around adults," the emphasis primarily falling on adults. For while one might presume that originality overrides any deficit of the recollective faculties, more often than not it marks memory's return in an unforeseen guise. Usually they could laugh off the slight attacks and raillery, but even the mildest comments hooked their self-perception like an angler's gaff. Any fellow can break a rule, and every fool will mend it. "Monkey, monkey, swinging from a tree, better run and hide or he'll jump on me." You beseeched them but they belittled this as mere unmanliness, sure any empathy might blunt the sharpness of your sorrow. Listening implies a desire to surrender. In one of his most spectacular fits, he confessed to having fathered other children during his libertine days, yet their resulting expressions barely altered their pre-formed masks of dismay. And yet what distinguished this moment from all of the others was the announcement that one of these too-numerous offenses had earned him a black-magic curse from the forsaken girl's mother. Good rhetoric always resurrects an argument. Hothouse. By propounding these theses and their concomitant antitheses, she subjected us to her usual welter of theories, and in so doing she appeared to have shrunk the polymorphous body of history into one monoeth(n)ic narrative so as to create a signifying medium that posed and answered all of its own questions. Huh. Blues, shoes, and a districtful of booze. In other words, private property and "propriety" are to the EuroAmerican bourgeois what the land and ancestors were to his other forebears, the fulcrum around which their entire sociopolitical view turned, and turns.

Intuition, Information, a Handy Index of Being

Gripping the chrysalis between the thumb and index finger you could divine the outlines of your future, for if such beauty might arise from a thing so hideous, you were persuaded that, despite your present, inelegant form, at least a few momentous transformations must await you. Out of nowhere. In back of the house sprawled the tree-nursery's dun and barren acres which had long since closed to commerce. To the neighborhood kids we claimed this as our own yard despite the blatantly red-tagged markers, until Ebony, our beloved Labrador retriever, fell dead from some herbicides the land's real owners had sprayed there. Behind the tool shed they retreated: behinds, bared teats. What would be sufficient under such trying circumstances. "Colored ABC Darians." Eventually a "camp" experience assumed the status of a "solution," though the reality of day camps, summer camps and scout camp depended on the year and their ever precarious finances. Prolonged exposure to sunlight will lead to yellowing or further surface degradation. Jumping double-dutch, till the night sky touched the ground, or jacks, but still the girls would play too fairly. Among our crew Kill the Man with the Ball prevailed or else a few rounds of Red Rover, and on days when there were only two of us, we might even resort to hopscotch. Each of them pined for a particular counselor, Kay M. being the one that he chose, for in spite of their snickers at her red hair and freckles, he found her laugh and wry spirit irresistible. Alone, and at best bereft. At scout camp the man was showering with his "sons," which sent a shudder of recognition up their spine. Numerous dissimilarities, however, distinguished the boys, yet in general they were thought to think as one. L'envie, envy. Written records exist as testimony beside the oral accounts of those present, as though the accumulation of all these voices would effect a kind of "explication." Who would cut such a big piece of the sweet-potato pie when so many good people in Africa go hungry. Peru, se compriende, is the country north of Chile and south of Colombia, he reread in those encyclopedias at the great-aunt's house, which not only listed Thailand as "Siam" but Zimbabwe as a colony called "Rhodesia." "If I were she," she corrected, digging sharply into your statement, to ensure that proper diction would take root. The source of oratory. Not infrequently some would express a yearning for a return to the era of the city's ascendancy, which was fitting as nostalgia rarely broaches the enigma of reason. Hiram R. Revels. In spite of the concatenation of family disasters they were still running with that bourgie crowd. A boon, apparently, when they won that all-expense-paid trip to Mexico, since, as that gossip announced to all around her at the luncheon, they both held such "menial jobs." Cotillion de León. How long would you be away from us, what would you bring us back, or would you decide to forsake us altogether. A lingering terror, an absence of breath. The parents, politically active in those heady days, eagerly lent their time and support, because that decent Irish family, and not the others they had come across, led the local corps of Democrats. Amid them, the middling ones. Shortly thereafter the actor assumed the nation's highest office, which precipitated the local organization's disintegration through anger, distrust, and apathy. "St. Louis Movement." With much fanfare, they commenced the beautillion militaire, which would be written up in all the Negro papers, and which he eschewed, to the dissatisfaction of certain relatives, out of an unexplained personal disinclination. In which affect becomes a guide and source, but to what: all, and nothing. The hurly-burly that ensued exceeded what we had expected, and yet we did not kowtow, but stood our unstable ground, knowing that later events, in which we determined our future, would bear such decisions out. Your feet are the very rotors that propel you through today, or on occasion two trusty harrows that render the moment around you fertile. Still no one could explain why on that side he had so many "grandfathers," who arrived and departed as regularly as the dun-notes. Mercy, mercy, me. "I'll turn my tail to the wind to make sure y'all have something to eat," thus who would dare to question the deeper contradictions in her reasoning. (Let's cool one) Which portended obliquely the theater of our future, but left to chance the curtain calls to come. They were horrified, however, that you could dredge up such minuscule details, since they had invested their reserves of faith in the telescopic movement of the years.

Words, Acts, a Search for Validation

From their perch on the telephone wires a choir of songbirds greeted him, thereby slaking his starved sensibilities with a scenario that the whiter months had withheld. Lily, thou gay and hardy flower. Geraniums, jotted in your curling stenographer's notebook, in "plastic graves on the windowsill," belied, as did the charging, mewling cat, the dispassion of the afternoon's unfolding. Never wearying of his records of these private adventures, he began to expend even longer hours on recondite projects, including the creation of a pseudo-African board game and a private linguistic mythopoetics. "I said put down that pen and pick up that football, and go out and play with the other boys," thus condemned, without jury, to the tribunal of the outdoors, the others. O oriole, oracle! Abstraction is a literal and figurative subtraction which incurs no net loss of value. In suburbia someone has to mow the lawn, of course, thus it fell within your purview, so you heaved and you hove, wrenching the mower along the slope, until it accidentally plunged into the sinkhole. Recriminations bloomed like shrapnel, as though the action, though an error, were a crime. Emprizes, for others more enterprising. Both poetry and fiction, however, find their roots in the act of making, a supposition grown gradually clearer as he explored the possibilities of reading. Upon your five-speed, across the asphalt, whirring as the blackbird flies. Dreams consequently assumed the contours, colors of the interior of the town's modest main library, where months seemingly elapsed as he maundered among the stacks, yet these reverie-journeys sometimes transmogrified into horrifying, recurrent nightmares in which, after each withdrawal of a careful selection of books, he arrived home to find himself either blind or illiterate. Such fears, though they initially seemed to possess an immobilizing permanence, disappeared amid the evanescence of each day's flux, a fact that displayed for him the shifting character of being, or phrased more prosaically, the process of the unreeling of the real. An alphabet, analphabet. All information will be kept confidential. Unlike that of our parish church, the Priory's plan was circular, with its white concrete parabolas by the Italian architect Neri and its collection of hand-crafted station altars, which usually seemed to be swathed in an otherworldly aroma of incense. Then his gaze would follow the black band of cassocks attenuating towards the entrance, entranced as he was by the stark and formal beauty of this relic of the ancient, Christian past. Silence poses a shrewder dilemma. Yet one had to endure the monks under other, more trying conditions, such as when they called upon one to conjugate the pluperfect subjunctive of the Latin verb "to bear," or to find the maximum and minimum areas of a football field. The essence of mathematics lies in these abilities to order and abstract. Aural, unreal. Our souls, consequently, are the assembly plants from which all passions emanate, but as we have come to recognize it is easier generally to list the classical passions of the soul than to define adequately either "passion" or "soul." Legei hoti touto alethes estin, a phrase he memorized so as to keep a good Greek motto at heart. Whatever flew up into the flue. Initially he would feign a stomach ache to gain his parents' sympathy, but alas, once this pattern had established itself, these pains became valid physiological crises. One should not, on the other hand, dismiss the portents of recurrent, minor aches. Elephant Rocks. In any case you were said to wield a vibrant, plastic tongue. Browsing as they had so many times at this particular local record store, they were trying to concentrate on the album and cassette-tape titles before them, but they could not shuck their nervousness at being stalked about the aisles by the floor and assistant managers. Pooseyite, hoosier. "Don't you ever turn your back to a nigger and a cash register," the cashier, thinking us out of earshot, asserted baldly. Esteem, mise en abîme. "A white freak like her is what I'm looking for now, y'all, 'cause when I was your age I had me quite a few," to which they wrinkled their mouths in disgust, the gestures a seal of their future. If you're light, you're all right, if you're brown, hang around, if you're black, get back. There are some taboos best left unbroken. Ask me now. Such expansive lyricism might be worthy of reprobation were not the very phenomenon of our lives a boundless source of poetry.

Inquiry as the Act of Living, Vital Improvisation

Missouri, being an amalgam of nearly every American region, presents the poet with a particularly useful analogue for an articulation of the "American," though close inspection shows a sum less metaphorically potent than its metonymically dissoluble parts. Show me. Having seen over four hundred skirmishes during the Civil War, the state ranked second only to Virginia in battle quantity, yet this factlet often receives scant mention in the most authoritative studies of that conflict. Yet with her Confederate government-in-exile and Republicanism on the wax, it was hard to keep up interest in the failing Southern cause. When later we spent a few days in Columbia, in Kansas City, in Jefferson City and the Ozark region, the breadth and diversity of the region's people and landscapes impressed themselves on us such that we vowed never again to reduce them to an anecdote. Shepherd of the Hills. And so, despite his urgings and the many texts they were poring through, they never discussed the implications of Duden's Report, the failed revolution of 1848, or the impact of the free blacks and their relationship with the Union Army in any class or forum, believing such trifles of the past at most a burden, and at the very least distasteful. A thirst for the trueness of lives and language, he anguishes ever. "Old Mazoo." More amusing always to prattle about the flailing baseball Cardinals, who, with the acquisition of Ozzie and Dale and Willie, and the stewardship of Whitey and Red, would reprise their winning ways within a year. To wit, intuit. "Salus populi suprema lex esto," uttered as much to contradict reality as to invoke it. In bygone years a community led by cooks and chauffeurs, carpenters, day laborers, and bootblacks, governed by ministers and Pullman porters, with that rare doctor or lawyer occupying the social summit. Knobnoster. By the time of the Miami riots they had selected new names and identities, thereby casting off another aspect of their oppressive heritage. The legacy as your grandfather and father had bequeathed it, which you rejected in favor of more compelling fantasy. Assembling all these puzzling pieces really requires the skills of a geographer-historian, which put his meager training and interests in some stead. Credit history for its luminous legerdemain, its adroit, unseen revisions, what the first six years write the next six erase, what one century pens with the most illuminative articulation, the consequent one hundred years transform into an entirely new text, unrecognizable at first glance. There but for the great hoax go our eyes. Having outgrown their former diversions, such as bike riding, crawfishing, and skateboarding, they locked themselves up in their rooms where they drew the shades before listening to records alone, or when not on the phone arranging dates and rendezvous, prowled the streets in someone's mother's car. Others might elect drugs as their chief form of recreation, though liquor was certifiably more common. This entails a decentered notion of the "subject." Reefer, rifer. The parents misread the signals or misconstrued each scene as they doggedly followed the trail of assignations. (Please wait for dial tone before inserting quarter.) The maliciousness of the storeclerks and the indifference of the teachers was later demonstrated to be part of a greater structural problem. Few, however, admit a predilection for improper relations of power, so as to present a front of probity, propriety. In the absence of a system of pure and unmediated signs, he nearly gave up on living altogether. Our recollective faculties extensively employ this function, dredging doggedly through the muck in search of that vital image. Free rides on the roller coaster and ridiculing the tourists from Iowa were the chief benefits of working at Six Flags, yet others who had traveled told of far more gravity-defying attractions and far more gullible targets elsewhere. The genius lies, *mendacity* in the execution. Bidding their co-workers adieu, he drove her home, where she begged him to come in, blow off a few hours, yet he declined, afraid she might be seeking more, for he had been warned innumerable times about their motives. Most lives are held together by this unspoken chain of commitments which we honor or break as the moment demands. "Now look here, baby, don't be wasting my time," as if one's presence alone were insufficient. Your spirit, a small fluorescent candle, never cedes to any circumstance its gleaming. Festival of Lights. Throughout he could recollect no negative references to Jews, though not because his parents rarely encountered them. Your recourse to a chain of corrections thereby functioned as a method of establishing certainty.

LITERATURE AS A GUIDE TO THE LIFE LIVED, A DELIVERANCE

On the template of night's sky they visually traced the constellations, which proved far more difficult to perform at home than they had witnessed at the planetarium. Thus, the worn yet lyric intensity of each evening's secret offering, what its occurrence might furnish beyond our small and sparsely lit furnace. Meate-chi-cippi. Lay teachers and priests, the latter becowled and armed with crisp, authentic British accents, appealed to the authority of the "Classical"

European tradition, now besieged with conflict to the point of internal sedition, like so much once imparted by "masters." Samuel Clemens. Throughout the boys a spirit of ridicule, beneath a veneer of respect, but only later would they fathom the immensity of their debt to these ill-paid, beleaguered pedagogues. Meachum Park. In the classroom Homer, Cicero, Melville, Tennyson, Hemingway, and Mauriac, while on the sly you perused Onstott, Heinlein, and Walker, yet those that would forge your aesthetic center in those formative years were Joyce, Tagore, Faulkner, and Morrison. Oozing, seething magma of presence, what I represents. "Gee, that's interesting, I had never noticed any patterns there," to which our silence was as much disproof as concurrence. Their theories to explain all manner of matter, though no theory to explain this thirst for theories. In the laboratory at the famous midwestern university, he prepared slides and learned the rudiments of neuroanatomy, sometimes growing giddy from the fumes of the rarefying benzene. Whereupon the accident with the microtome, which they shied away from shaping into a lawsuit. "J'averterai Bill dès qu'il sera revenu," repeat it, to impress them. Ultimately although some tired of bandying about "Nigger Jim" or "pickanines" before him, most were reveling in the new climate of conservatism, which introduced far more subtle ways of impressing upon others one's social and economic superiority. Time had come to begin applying to college, the next step to which the aspirations of their class had most logically led. Please remove seal before opening. "Harvard don't keep on folks who can't pay or charm their way!"

she cackled, her face a cracking, crackling lantern. Who would leave the city of one's birth without hesitation, lest one suffocate under the swaddle of so much past. Convogosa. The strain of our ruse quite rightly blinded us, until we lost sight of who we truly were. Many of them now worked at the post office, which had become such a trying job. One must, in other words, eventually come to terms with the provisional. According to the standards the images conveyed, your appearance was grotesquely disharmonic. High butt, narrow hips, broad shoulders, full lips. As a result you cut the cake or stollen into minuscule pieces, aiming to perfect yourself, yet deep down you knew the real reason behind your actions was to savor more fully each morsel. In this way a sense of economy developed, whose flip side became an inability to see the larger picture. "Happy Days." Now you must talk up our quarrel. It is foolish, the perceptive film theorist noted, for them to invoke post-modernity when as a people they appear to have been bypassed by the modern. Besides, dialogue has proven so woefully insufficient, though we continue to invest our energies in it. Your cognizance linked these as a chain of incidents, closer observation made clear their antecedents, but what you sought, like any artist, were the very events themselves. St. Louis Blues. Afterwards, we dispersed to our pre-appointed stations in society, with many becoming doctors, bankers, or mechanics. This naturally obviated the need for friendly contact or regular, intimate phone calls. Hindsight is often crueler than an unforgiving lover; perfidy is the knife that wounds far more deeply than others. The parents were still whispering something about those two, which lent this all an aura of shame. Always the desire to be loved formed the nucleus, about which other events and moments, positive, negative, or otherwise, whirred like the elementary particles. Some men, women, certain trees, bare certainties. Were these accounts, as was projected for this aesthetic project, selected and set down as carefully as tesseracts, the cumulative effect would approximate that of a living, dazzling, eighteen-panel mosaic. Given the general trends towards ignorance and indifference, however, no one thought to challenge his methods, let alone his motives. We took turns reciting poems by the Black Arts poets from one of those volumes now growing dusty on the godmother's bookshelves. "Man, you don't even know the scrapple from the apple, and you ain't gon' get that out no old dead cracker's book," our reply a prolonged, anguished stare into a portrait of life dissolving before us. Thus his musings, when written down, gradually melded, gathered shape, solidified like a well-mixed mâché, and thus, upon rereading them he realized what he had accomplished was the construction of an actual voice. The final dances of youth, dim incandescence. Willow weep for me. And so, patient reader, these remarks should be duly noted as a series of mere life-notes aspiring to the condition of annotations.

Boston–Dorchester–St. Louis–Charlottesville
1992–1994

References & Notes

REFERENCES

Collins, Earl A., *Folk Tales of Missouri*, Christopher Publishing House: Boston, 1935.

Foley, William E., *A History of Missouri, 1673 to 1820*, University of Missouri Press: Columbia, 1971.

Franklin, John Hope, *From Slavery to Freedom*, Vintage: New York, 1969.

Lipsitz, George, *A Life in the Struggle: Ivory Perry and the Culture of Opposition*, Temple University Press: Philadelphia, 1988.

March, David D., *A History of Missouri* (4 vols.), University of Chicago Press: Chicago, 1967.

Marsh, Sarah Louise, and Charles G. Vannest, *Missouri Anthology*, Christopher Publishing House: Boston, 1932.

Olson, Audrey L., *St. Louis Germans, 1850–1920*, Arno Press: New York, 1980.

Peper, Christian B., Ed., *An Historian's Conscience: The Correspondence of Arnold J. Toynbee and Columba Cary-Elwes, Monk of Ampleforth*, Beacon Press: Boston, 1986.

Primm, James Neal, *The Lion of the Valley: St. Louis, Missouri*, Pruett Publishing Company: Boulder, 1990.

NOTES

pages

5   Rudipoots: A colloquialism akin to "ghettoheads," meaning an ignorant or foolish person.

7   Chatillon-DeMenil: This refers specifically to the historic mansion and tourist site in south St. Louis that once housed the family of Dr. Nicholas de Menil, a prominent resident of the nineteenth century, and more broadly to the era of St. Louis's ascendancy.

8   Aos pés da cruz : A Pinto Gonçalves tune, as played by Miles Davis, a native East St. Louisan, with Gil Evans and orchestra, in a Columbia recording from the 1960s. "Aos pés da cruz," a Portuguese phrase, translates into English as "at the foot of the cross."

9   Ring-A-Levio: A common children's game in which members of one group try to find and capture hidden members of another group.

10   Poinciana: An ornamental shrub commonly found in the West Indies; also the title of a song by Simon and Bernier, played exquisitely by Ahmad Jamal on his Pershing Lounge session of 1958.

13   Chain of Rocks: A series of bluffs, with a park, overlooking the Mississippi River north of St. Louis City.

13   Treemonisha: A 1905 opera by Scott Joplin, written while he was resident in Sedalia, MO, and not premiered until 1972, in Atlanta, GA. The theme of the opera is the salvation of the Black race through education, and Treemonisha, a young woman, is the protagonist.

17   Aleikam salaam: Arabic for "And peace be with you," the traditional reply to a greeting.

25   La Ba-Kair: The French popular nickname for the great Josephine Baker, a native St. Louisan.

27   Raus, Ihr kleine Mäuser, raus: German for "Get out of here, you little mice, get out of here!"

27   Juneteenth: In the Midwest and South(west), this celebration, usually June 17, commemorates the day when slaves of those regions learned they were no longer in bondage.

31	Pannonica: The title of a serene Charlie Parker composition, named after the Baroness Pannonica de Koenigswarter, a Jazz patroness of some renown, in whose apartment Parker died in 1955.
32	Turner's Hall *Turnverein*: A St. Louis based German gymnastic society, whose small arsenal and membership would form part of the Unionist "Home Guard" organized by Samuel Blair in pre-Civil War St. Louis.
34	Asafetida : A malodorous medicinal gum, believed to ward off illness, that was sometimes placed in a sack or bag and strapped around the neck of Southern black children.
34	Evonce: A composition by Danny Quebec West and Idrees Sulieman, played by Thelonious Monk and his combo in a Blue Note recording from the 1940s.
37	Carondelet: The name of the city, founded in 1767, avenue, commons and park in the St. Louis area. Baron de Carondelet in 1793 organized the (re)settlement of the native Indians in Louisiana territory.
39	Bakai: A composition by Cal Massey, as played by Jazz visionary John Coltrane and a sextet on a Prestige recording from the late 1950s. According to the liner notes by Ira Gitler, "Bakai," an Arabic term, translates as "cry" in English.
40	Palmares: The great city established by escaped slaves, or *quilombo*, in the seventeenth century in northeastern Brazil. Palmares was also known as the "Black Troy."
46	Klactoveededstene: A composition by Jazz trumpeter and bandleader Dizzie Gillespie.
53	Grumio erat coquus: Latin for "Grumio was the cook." An adaptation of a line from the early levels in the Cambridge Latin Series.
55	Schneeblick: German for "snowglance, snowgaze." A neologism, after Paul Celan.
57	I'n-Shta-Heh: Little Osage for "Heavy eyebrows," the name given to the French colonizers.
58	Marronage: French, for the condition of being a *marron*, or runaway/escaped slave, in a francophone nation or colony, such as Haiti before 1804.
69	Legei hoti touto alethes estin: Ancient Greek for "He says this all to be the truth."

72 Salus populi suprema lex esto: Latin for "Let the welfare of the people be the supreme law," the official motto of Missouri.

75 Meate-chi-cippi: The Algonkian name for the Mississippi River, it means "Father of the Waters."

77 Convogosa: A brave mythic Illinois chief whose courageous stand in self-defense supposedly left the "Footprint on the Rocks" in southwestern Illinois across the Mississippi from St. Louis.

New Directions Paperbacks—A Partial Listing

Walter Abish, *How German Is It.* NDP508.
Ahmed Ali, *Twilight in Delhi.* NDP782.
John Allman, *Scenarios for a Mixed Landscape.* NDP619.
Alfred Andersch, *Efraim's Book.* NDP779.
Sherwood Anderson, *Poor White.* NDP763.
Wayne Andrews, *The Surrealist Parade.* NDP689.
David Antin, *Tuning.* NDP570.
G. Apollinaire, *Selected Writings.*† NDP310.
Jimmy S. Baca, *Martín & Meditations.* NDP648.
 Black Mesa Poems. NDP676.
Djuna Barnes, *Nightwood.* NDP98.
J. Barzun, *An Essay on French Verse.* NDP708
H. E. Bates, *Elephant's Nest in a Rhubarb Tree.* NDP669.
 A Party for the Girls. NDP653.
Charles Baudelaire, *Flowers of Evil.* †NDP684.
 Paris Spleen. NDP294.
Bei Dao, *Old Snow.* NDP727.
 Waves. NDP693.
Gottfried Benn, *Primal Vision.* NDP322.
Adolfo Bioy Casares, *A Russian Doll.* NDP745.
Carmel Bird, *The Bluebird Café.* NDP707.
Johannes Bobrowski, *Shadow Lands.* NDP788.
Wolfgang Borchert, *The Man Outside.* NDP319.
Jorge Luis Borges, *Labyrinths.* NDP186.
 Seven Nights. NDP576.
Kay Boyle, *The Crazy Hunter.* NDP770.
 Fifty Stories. NDP741.
Kamau Brathwaite, *MiddlePassages.* NDP776.
M. Bulgakov, *Flight & Bliss.* NDP593.
 The Life of M. de Moliere. NDP601.
Frederick Busch, *Absent Friends.* NDP721.
Veza Canetti, *Yellow Street.* NDP709.
Ernesto Cardenal, *Zero Hour.* NDP502.
Joyce Cary, *Mister Johnson.* NDP631.
Hayden Carruth, *Tell Me Again. . . .* NDP677.
Camilo José Cela, *Mazurka for Two Dead Men.* NDP789.
Louis-Ferdinand Céline,
 Death on the Installment Plan. NDP330.
 Journey to the End of the Night. NDP542.
René Char. *Selected Poems.* †NDP734.
Jean Cocteau, *The Holy Terrors.* NDP212.
M. Collis, *She Was a Queen.* NDP716.
Gregory Corso, *Long Live Man.* NDP127.
 Herald of the Autochthonic Spirit. NDP522.
Robert Creeley, *Memory Gardens.* NDP613.
 Windows. NDP687.
Margaret Dawe, *Nissequott.* NDP775.
Osamu Dazai, *The Setting Sun.* NDP258.
 No Longer Human. NDP357.
Mme. de Lafayette, *The Princess of Cleves.* NDP660.
E. Dujardin, *We'll to the Woods No More.* NDP682.
Robert Duncan, *Selected Poems.* NDP754.
Wm. Empson, *7 Types of Ambiguity.* NDP204
 Some Versions of Pastoral. NDP92.
S. Endo, *The Sea and the Poison.* NDP737.
Wm. Everson, *The Residual Years.* NDP263.
Lawrence Ferlinghetti, *A Coney Island of the Mind.* NDP74.
 These Are My Rivers. NDP786.
 Wild Dreams of a New Beginning. NDP663.
Ronald Firbank, *Five Novels.* NDP581.
 Three More Novels. NDP614.
F. Scott Fitzgerald, *The Crack-up.* NDP757.
Gustave Flaubert, *Dictionary.* NDP230.
J. Gahagan, *Did Gustav Mahler Ski?* NDP711.
Gandhi, *Ghandi on Non-Violence.* NDP197.
Gary, Romain, *Promise at Dawn.* NDP635.
 The Life Before Us ("Madame Rosa"). NDP604.
W. Gerhardie, *Futility.* NDP722.
Goethe, *Faust*, Part I. NDP70.
Allen Grossman, *The Ether Dome.* NDP723.
Martin Grzimek, *Shadowlife.* NDP705.

Guigonnat, Henri, *Daemon in Lithuania.* NDP592.
Lars Gustafsson, *The Death of a Beekeeper.* NDP523.
 A Tiler's Afternoon. NDP761.
John Hawkes, *The Beetle Leg.* NDP239.
 Second Skin. NDP146.
Samuel Hazo, *To Paris.* NDP512.
H. D. *Collected Poems.* NDP611.
 Helen in Egypt. NDP380.
 HERmione. NDP526.
 Selected Poems. NDP658.
 Tribute to Freud. NDP572.
Robert E. Helbling. *Heinrich von Kleist.* NDP390.
William Herrick, *Bradovich.* NDP762.
Herman Hesse, *Siddhartha.* NDP65.
Paul Hoover, *The Novel.* NDP706.
Susan Howe, *The Nonconformist's Memorial.* NDP755.
Vicente Huidobro, *Selected Poetry.* NDP520.
C. Isherwood, *All the Conspirators.* NDP480.
 The Berlin Stories. NDP134.
Lêdo Ivo, *Snake's Nest.* NDP521.
Fleur Jaeggy, *Sweet Days of Discipline.* NDP758.
Henry James, *The Sacred Fount.* NDP790.
Gustav Janouch, *Conversations with Kafka.* NDP313.
Alfred Jarry, *Ubu Roi.* NDP105.
Robinson Jeffers, *Cawdor and Medea.* NDP293.
B. S. Johnson, *Christie Malry's. . . .* NDP600.
James Joyce, *Stephen Hero.* NDP133.
Franz Kafka, *Amerika.* NDP117.
Mary Karr, *The Devil's Tour.* NDP768.
Bob Kaufman, *The Ancient Rain.* NDP514.
H. von Kleist, *Prince Friedrich.* NDP462.
Dezsö Kosztolányi, *Anna Édes.* NDP772.
Rüdiger Kremer, *The Color of Snow.* NDP743.
Jules Laforgue, *Moral Tales.* NDP594.
P. Lal, *Great Sanskrit Plays.* NDP142.
Tommaso Landolfi, *Gogol's Wife.* NDP155.
D. Larsen, *Stitching Porcelain.* NDP710.
James Laughlin, *The Man in the Wall.* NDP759.
Lautréamont, *Maldoror.* NDP207.
H. Leibowitz, *Fabricating Lives.* NDP715.
Siegfried Lenz, *The German Lesson.* NDP618.
Denise Levertov, *Breathing the Water.* NDP640.
 A Door in the Hive. NDP685.
 Evening Train. NDP750.
 New & Selected Essays. NDP749.
 Poems 1960–1967. NDP549.
 Poems 1968–1972. NDP629.
 Oblique Prayers. NDP578.
Harry Levin, *James Joyce.* NDP87.
Li Ch'ing-chao, *Complete Poems.* NDP492.
Enrique Lihn, *The Dark Room.* †NDP542.
C. Lispector, *Soulstorm.* NDP671.
 The Hour of the Star. NDP733.
García Lorca, *Five Plays.* NDP232.
 The Public & Play Without a Title. NDP561.
 Selected Poems. †NDP114.
 Three Tragedies. NDP52.
Francisco G. Lorca, *In The Green Morning.* NDP610.
Michael McClure, *Simple Eyes.* NDP780.
Carson McCullers, *The Member of the Wedding.* (Playscript) NDP153.
X. de Maistre, *Voyage Around My Room.* NDP791.
Stéphane Mallarme,† *Selected Poetry and Prose.* NDP529.
Bernadette Mayer, *A Bernadette Mayer Reader.* NDP739.
Thomas Merton, *Asian Journal.* NDP394.
 New Seeds of Contemplation. NDP337.
 Selected Poems. NDP85.
 Thomas Merton in Alaska. NDP652.
 The Way of Chuang Tzu. NDP276.
 Zen and the Birds of Appetite. NDP261.
Henri Michaux, *A Barbarian in Asia.* NDP622.
 Selected Writings. NDP264.
Henry Miller, *The Air-Conditioned Nightmare.* NDP302.
 Aller Retour New York. NDP753.

For complete listing request free catalog from
New Directions, 80 Eighth Avenue, New York 10011   †Bilingual

Big Sur & The Oranges. NDP161.
The Colossus of Maroussi. NDP75.
A Devil in Paradise. NDP765.
Into the Heart of Life. NDP728.
The Smile at the Foot of the Ladder. NDP386.
Y. Mishima, *Confessions of a Mask*. NDP253.
Death in Midsummer. NDP215.
Frédéric Mistral, *The Memoirs*. NDP632.
Eugenio Montale, *It Depends*.† NDP507.
Selected Poems.† NDP193.
Paul Morand, *Fancy Goods/Open All Night*. NDP567.
Vladimir Nabokov, *Nikolai Gogol*. NDP78.
Laughter in the Dark. NDP729.
The Real Life of Sebastian Knight. NDP432.
P. Neruda, *The Captain's Verses*.† NDP345.
Residence on Earth.† NDP340.
Fully Empowered. NDP792.
New Directions in Prose & Poetry (Anthology).
Available from #17 forward to #55.
Robert Nichols, *Arrival*. NDP437.
Exile. NDP485.
J. F. Nims, *The Six-Cornered Snowflake*. NDP700.
Charles Olson, *Selected Writings*. NDP231.
Toby Olson, *The Life of Jesus*. NDP417.
George Oppen, *Collected Poems*. NDP418.
István Örkeny, *The Flower Show/
The Toth Family*. NDP536.
Wilfred Owen, *Collected Poems*. NDP210.
José Emilio Pacheco, *Battles in the Desert*. NDP637.
Selected Poems.† NDP638.
Nicanor Parra, *Antipoems: New & Selected*. NDP603.
Boris Pasternak, *Safe Conduct*. NDP77.
Kenneth Patchen, *Because It Is*. NDP83.
Collected Poems. NDP284.
Selected Poems. NDP160.
Ota Pavel, *How I Came to Know Fish*. NDP713.
Octavio Paz, *Collected Poems*. NDP719.
Configurations.† NDP303.
A Draft of Shadows.† NDP489.
Selected Poems. NDP574.
Sunstone.† NDP735.
A Tree Within.† NDP661.
St. John Perse, *Selected Poems*.† NDP545.
Ezra Pound, *ABC of Reading*. NDP89.
Confucius. NDP285.
Confucius to Cummings. (Anth.) NDP126.
Diptych Rome-London. NDP783.
A Draft of XXX Cantos. NDP690.
Elektra. NDP683.
Guide to Kulchur. NDP257.
Literary Essays. NDP250.
Personae. NDP697.
Selected Cantos. NDP304.
Selected Poems. NDP66.
The Spirit of Romance. NDP266.
Eça de Queiroz, *Ilustrious House of Ramires*. NDP785.
Raymond Queneau, *The Blue Flowers*. NDP595.
Exercises in Style. NDP513.
Mary de Rachewiltz, *Ezra Pound*. NDP405.
Raja Rao, *Kanthapura*. NDP224.
Herbert Read, *The Green Child*. NDP208.
P. Reverdy, *Selected Poems*.† NDP346.
Kenneth Rexroth, *An Autobiographical Novel*. NDP725.
Classics Revisited. NDP621.
More Classics Revisited. NDP668.
Flower Wreath Hill. NDP724.
100 Poems from the Chinese. NDP192.
100 Poems from the Japanese.† NDP147.
Selected Poems. NDP581.
Women Poets of China. NDP528.
Women Poets of Japan. NDP527.
Rainer Maria Rilke, *Poems from
The Book of Hours*. NDP408.
Possibility of Being. (Poems). NDP436.
Where Silence Reigns. (Prose). NDP464.
Arthur Rimbaud. *Illuminations*.† NDP56.
Season in Hell & Drunken Boat.† NDP97.
Edouard Roditi, *Delights of Turkey*. NDP445.

Jerome Rothenberg, *Khurbn*. NDP679.
The Lorca Variations. NDP771.
Nayantara Sahgal, *Rich Like Us*. NDP665.
Ihara Saikaku, *The Life of an Amorous Woman*. NDP270.
St. John of the Cross, *Poems*.† NDP341.
W. Saroyan, *Fresno Stories*. NDP793.
Jean-Paul Sartre, *Nausea*. NDP82.
The Wall (Intimacy). NDP272.
P. D. Scott, *Crossing Borders*. NDP796.
Listening to the Candle. NDP747.
Delmore Schwartz, *Selected Poems*. NDP241.
In Dreams Begin Responsibilities. NDP454.
Hasan Shah, *The Dancing Girl*. NDP777.
K. Shiraishi, *Seasons of Sacred Lust*. NDP453.
Stevie Smith, *Collected Poems*. NDP562.
Novel on Yellow Paper. NDP778.
Gary Snyder, *The Back Country*. NDP249.
The Real Work. NDP499.
Turtle Island. NDP381.
Muriel Spark, *The Comforters*. NDP796.
The Driver's Seat. NDP786.
The Public Image. NDP767.
Enid Starkie, *Rimbaud*. NDP254.
Stendhal, *Three Italian Chronicles*. NDP704.
Antonio Tabucchi, *Indian Nocturne*. NDP666.
Nathaniel Tarn, *Lyrics . . . Bride of God*. NDP391.
Dylan Thomas, *Adventures in Skin Trade*. NDP183.
A Child's Christmas in Wales. NDP181.
Collected Poems 1934–1952. NDP316.
Collected Stories. NDP626.
Portrait of the Artist as a Young Dog. NDP51.
Quite Early One Morning. NDP90.
Under Milk Wood. NDP73.
Tian Wen: *A Chinese Book of Origins*. NDP624.
Uwe Timm, *The Snake Tree*. NDP686.
Lionel Trilling, *E. M. Forster*. NDP189.
Tu Fu, *Selected Poems*. NDP675.
N. Tucci, *The Rain Came Last*. NDP688.
Paul Valéry, *Selected Writings*.† NDP184.
Elio Vittorini, *A Vittorini Omnibus*. NDP366.
Rosmarie Waldrop, *A Key into the Language of America*. NDP798.
Robert Penn Warren, *At Heaven's Gate*. NDP588.
Eliot Weinberger, *Outside Stories*. NDP751.
Nathanael West, *Miss Lonelyhearts &
Day of the Locust*. NDP125.
J. Wheelwright, *Collected Poems*. NDP544.
Tennessee Williams, *Baby Doll*. NDP714.
Cat on a Hot Tin Roof. NDP398.
Collected Stories. NDP784.
The Glass Menagerie. NDP218.
Hard Candy. NDP225.
A Lovely Sunday for Creve Coeur. NDP497.
One Arm & Other Stories. NDP237.
Red Devil Battery Sign. NDP650.
The Roman Spring of Mrs. Stone. NDP770.
A Streetcar Named Desire. NDP501.
Sweet Bird of Youth. NDP409.
Twenty-Seven Wagons Full of Cotton. NDP217.
Vieux Carre. NDP482.
William Carlos Williams.
Asphodel. NDP794.
The Autobiography. NDP223.
Collected Poems: Vol. I. NDP730.
Collected Poems: Vol. II. NDP731.
The Doctor Stories. NDP585.
Imaginations. NDP329.
In The American Grain. NDP53.
In The Money. NDP240.
Paterson. Complete. NDP152.
Pictures from Brueghel. NDP118.
Selected Poems (new ed.). NDP602.
White Mule. NDP226.
Wisdom Books:
St. Francis. NDP477; *Taoists*. NDP509;
Wisdom of the Desert. NDP295; *Zen Masters*.
NDP415.

For complete listing request free catalog from
New Directions, 80 Eighth Avenue, New York 10011

†Bilingual